STAR WARS™

EPISODE I

THE PHANTOM MENACE

This book belongs to

....

Acknowledgments

Special thanks to Lucasfilm Ltd for their invaluable assistance
and for providing the artwork for this book.

First published in the UK in 2024 by Studio Press Books,
an imprint of Bonnier Books UK,
4th Floor, Victoria House, Bloomsbury Square,
London WC1B 4DA
Owned by Bonnier Books,
Sveavägen 56, Stockholm, Sweden
bonnierbooks.co.uk

Printed in China
1 3 5 7 9 10 8 6 4 2

Text adapted by Tom Huddleston
Edited by Emil Fortune
Designed by Maddox Philpot
Cover illustrated by Alexander Ward
Production by Nick Read

A CIP catalogue record is available from the British Library

We waited 16 years for more Star Wars films. It wasn't until The Phantom Menace premiered in 1999 that we finally had the chance to learn all about what happened before the original trilogy and experience what George Lucas had in store for this new chapter of Star Wars movies.

Since the release of *Return of the Jedi*, I had attended art school and had worked in various agencies as a graphic designer and art director. I worked on movie posters, advertising and entertainment design, and even spent a few years in Hollywood at the agency that designed the *Star Wars* logo and all of the original *Star Wars* movie posters.

While working in San Francisco as an art director designing music merchandise, I heard that George Lucas was writing new *Star Wars* stories. Lucasfilm was working on a prequel trilogy and they were looking for an art director for the merchandise division. It took me many months – and I almost gave up – but I finally prevailed and landed my dream job at Skywalker Ranch with Lucasfilm. All of it felt otherworldly. I was working with and in the presence of visionaries and people that I had idolized and read about for many years.

The Phantom Menace was all about Anakin Skywalker, the future Jedi with special abilities; his Jedi mentors, Qui-Gon Jinn and a young Obi-Wan Kenobi; beautiful Queen Amidala; and a striking villain, Darth Maul, with his double-bladed lightsaber and graphic face markings. The film introduced brand new planets and vehicles, characters and creatures, and armies of droids. From high speed podracing and Jar Jar Binks hi-jinks to epic lightsaber and space battles, it was a new *Star Wars* for new generations. That in and of itself was so exciting to everyone involved.

This new retelling features drawings and paintings that ushered in this new trilogy. These incredible artists brought a new look to an established franchise. It attracted a young audience who could adopt *Star Wars* as their own. And therein lies the beauty of these films: there truly is something for everyone.

Troy Alders
Art Director, Lucasfilm

The planet Naboo, as seen from orbit. **BRIAN FLORA / DIGITAL MATTE PAINTING**

For over a thousand years, the Galactic Republic had known peace, under the guidance of the Senate and its Supreme Chancellor, and aided by those noble guardians of truth and justice, the Knights of the Jedi Order.

But then a new danger arose. Angered by some of the Senate's decisions, a powerful group known as the Trade Federation invaded the peaceful world of Naboo. Their battleships orbited the planet, preventing any other starships from landing. They were determined to force the Senate to listen to their demands.

In the Republic capital on Coruscant, senators from across the galaxy debated the problem, and argued over how they should respond. But Chancellor Valorum knew that the matter was too urgent. Acting in secret, he sent two Jedi to Naboo to speak to the Trade Federation and reach an agreement.

One of the Jedi was a wise and experienced master named Qui-Gon Jinn, who had been a member of the Jedi Order for many years. The other was his youthful apprentice, or Padawan: Obi-Wan Kenobi, who had been raised in the great Jedi Temple on Coruscant.

A costume concept for the Jedi Knight, Qui-Gon Jinn. **Iain McCaig / Pencil**

The two Jedi took a small cruiser to Naboo and landed inside the huge Trade Federation battleship. There they were greeted by a silver protocol droid who took them to a small chamber to await the arrival of the head of the Trade Federation, Viceroy Nute Gunray.

'I have a bad feeling about this,' Obi-Wan told his master, sensing danger. The Jedi were able to use a mystical energy field known as the Force to heighten their abilities.

A costume concept for the Padawan, Obi-Wan Kenobi. **Iain McCaig / Marker**

But Qui-Gon told his Padawan to stay focused. 'Keep your concentration here and now, where it belongs.'

Obi-Wan wondered how the viceroy would react to the arrival of two Jedi on his ship. Would he be frightened, or would he be angry? But Qui-Gon wasn't concerned. 'These Federation types are cowards,' he said. 'The negotiations will be short.'

Qui-Gon was correct. Nute Gunray was a coward. On the battleship's main bridge, the viceroy had just learned that the two ambassadors were Jedi. Shaking with fear, he sent a transmission to a mysterious figure known as Darth Sidious and asked him what to do.

'We must accelerate our plans. Begin landing your troops,' Sidious commanded. As for the Jedi, Sidious told the Viceroy to have them killed immediately! Gunray was shocked, but he was even more afraid of Sidious than he was of the Jedi. He agreed to do as his master ordered.

Without warning, a blast of laser fire destroyed the space cruiser that had brought the Jedi to Naboo. Sensing their peril, Qui-Gon and Obi-Wan leapt to their feet and drew their lightsabers. They each took a deep breath as deadly poison gas flooded into the sealed chamber.

Outside the locked room, a squad of Trade Federation battle droids had been sent to make sure that the Jedi were dead. But when the doors opened the Jedi burst out, using their lightsabers to repel the droids' blaster fire. With the help of the Force, they quickly defeated the droids and went in search of the treacherous viceroy.

On the bridge, Nute Gunray cowered in terror. As Obi-Wan fought off the battle droids, Qui-Gon used his lightsaber to try to cut through the thick metal blast door to the bridge.

Concept art for the Neimoidian Viceroy, Nute Gunray. **Iain McCaig / Marker**

Concept art for droideka 'destroyer droids'. **DOUG CHIANG / MARKER**

But when they were attacked by a pair of heavily armed and shielded droidekas, the Jedi were forced to retreat.

Sneaking through the ventilation shafts, the Jedi were able to reach the ship's hangar, where they found thousands of battle droids preparing to land on Naboo. Qui-Gon decided that they should slip aboard one of the landing craft, travel down to the planet and warn its people of the Trade Federation's plans.

'Well, you were right about one thing, Master,' Obi-Wan said with a smile. 'The negotiations were short.'

In the grand throne room of
Naboo's Royal Palace, the young
Queen Amidala was speaking with
her advisors. Despite her humble
background, Amidala had been chosen
to rule by the people of Naboo. It was
a responsibility that she took
very seriously.

Viceroy Gunray had told the queen
that the two Jedi never arrived
on his ship. Now she had
received a transmission
from Naboo's Senator
Palpatine, a very clever man
whom the queen trusted
completely. Palpatine said
he was sure the Jedi had
made it, but before he
could say any more the
signal was cut off.

'A communications
disruption can only
mean one thing,' insisted
Governor Sio Bibble.
'Invasion!'

Concept for Nute Gunray featuring a Neimoidian
walking chair. **DOUG CHIANG / MARKER**

But Queen Amidala was reluctant to believe him. 'The Federation would not dare go that far,' she said. 'I will not condone a course of action that will lead us to war.' Little did she know that the war had already come.

In the forests of Naboo, the droid army had begun landing their ships and unloading their huge multi-troop transports. The noise of their arrival terrified the local wildlife, sending herds of animals crashing through the trees. Running alongside them was Qui-Gon Jinn, who had stowed away aboard one of the droid ships.

Ahead of him Qui-Gon saw a peculiar being, waving his arms fearfully as he tried to avoid a speeding troop transport. Qui-Gon grabbed him and

Trade Federation Multi Troop Transports on Naboo. **DOUG CHIANG / ACRYLIC ON ILLUSTRATION BOARD**

pushed him to the ground as the transport thundered over their heads.

The being was a Gungan, a long-eared native of the planet Naboo. His name was Jar Jar Binks, and he was very thankful to Qui-Gon for saving his life. He swore that from now on, he would be Qui-Gon's servant.

As Obi-Wan joined his master, Jar Jar informed them that the safest place to hide from the droid army would be Gunga City, a secret location known only to his people. Unfortunately, Jar Jar had been banished from the city and did not dare go back.

Qui-Gon frowned. 'Do you hear that?' he asked, as the roar of the droid army echoed through the forest. 'That is the sound of a thousand terrible things heading this way.' Jar Jar gulped and agreed to show the Jedi the way to his former home.

Concept for Jar Jar Binks. **TERRYL WHITLACH / MARKER**

As night fell, he led them to a misty shore. The Gungan leapt into the water, gesturing to his new friends to follow him. Wearing special underwater breathing devices, the Jedi swam down into the depths.

There they came across an incredible sight. The city of the Gungans was made up of hundreds of underwater spheres, each one glowing with a golden light. Inside, the Jedi were able to remove their breathing devices, and they were taken before Boss Nass, the most powerful of all the Gungans.

Concept art for Jar Jar Binks. **DOUG CHIANG / ACRYLIC ON ILLUSTRATION BOARD**

Boss Nass was aware of the droid army, but he did not want to help the Jedi. In those days, there was little friendship between the Gungans and the human population who lived on the surface of Naboo.

Concept art for the Gungan underwater city, Otoh Gunga. **DOUG CHIANG / ACRYLIC ON ILLUSTRATION BOARD**

Obi-Wan tried to reason with him that the humans' fate and that of the Gungans was intertwined. 'What happens to one of you will affect the other,' he said. But Boss Nass was too stubborn, so Qui-Gon used a Jedi mind trick to convince him to help them. He also persuaded Nass to allow Jar Jar to go with them, as their guide.

Piloting a Gungan submarine known as a bongo, the Jedi and their fearful friend set out for Naboo's capital city, taking a direct but dangerous

Concept for the Gungan leader Boss Nass. **ED NATIVIDAD / PENCIL**

route through the planet's core. In the depths of the ocean, they were almost eaten by a giant gooberfish and a huge colo clawfish, but the bongo reached the city of Theed in one piece.

Unfortunately, the Jedi were too late. Led by Viceroy Nute Gunray, the Trade Federation had occupied Theed and taken Queen Amidala prisoner.

Concept art for the underwater sequence featuring the Bongo sub and a pursuing opee sea killer.
DOUG CHIANG / ACRYLIC PAINTING

'I will not cooperate,' the defiant queen told the viceroy.

Gunray did not believe her. He ordered his droid soldiers to take the queen away, along with her advisors and handmaidens. But the droids were ambushed by the Jedi, who freed the captives and took them safely to the palace's main hangar, where they found the Royal Starship waiting.

The Queen had no wish to abandon her people, but Qui-Gon Jinn insisted that her life would be in danger if she did not flee. 'There is something else behind all this, Your Highness,' he said firmly. 'There is no logic in the Federation's move here. My feelings tell me they will destroy you.'

Knowing the risks, the queen turned to her trusted handmaiden, Padmé. 'We are brave, Your Highness,' the young woman assured her. The queen nodded, and agreed to leave with the Jedi.

Obi-Wan and Qui-Gon destroyed the droids who were patrolling the hangar and hurried the queen and her companions aboard the sleek Royal Starship. Piloted by Commander Ric Olié, the ship left the hangar and headed for the blackness of space.

Concept art for Queen Amidala. **Iain McCaig / Marker**

There they found the Trade Federation's mighty battleships waiting for them. A direct hit destroyed the

Royal Starship's shields, leaving them vulnerable to enemy fire. But a brave little astromech droid named R2-D2 was able to fix the problem just in time, allowing the ship to escape.

The Royal Starship's hyperdrive was also damaged in the battle, which meant they would be unable to reach Coruscant. Obi-Wan suggested that they land on the nearby world of Tatooine, a remote desert planet under the control of the notorious gangsters known as the Hutts. The queen's head of security, Captain Panaka, thought this was a bad idea, but Qui-Gon urged Amidala to trust him.

Back on Naboo, Viceroy Gunray was forced to admit to Darth Sidious that Queen Amidala had escaped. Sidious decided to send his own apprentice, a fearsome Dathomirian warrior named Darth Maul, to hunt down the queen and kill anyone who protected her.

Concept art of the Naboo Royal Starship escaping the blockade. DOUG CHIANG / ACRYLIC PAINTING

Costume concept for Darth Maul.
IAIN McCAIG / MARKER

Darth Maul smiled cruelly. 'At last we will reveal ourselves to the Jedi,' he told his master. 'At last we will have revenge.'

As the Royal Starship approached Tatooine, Qui-Gon told Ric Olié to land on the outskirts of a large settlement, where he hoped to be able to buy a new hyperdrive. But the Jedi Master had become aware of a disturbance in the Force, and before he left, he warned Obi-Wan to stay on his guard, and protect the queen.

As Qui-Gon led Jar Jar Binks and R2-D2 away through the dunes, a voice called out to them. Looking back, Qui-Gon saw Captain Panaka following with Padmé. 'Her Highness commands you to take her handmaiden with you,' Panaka told the Jedi.

Qui-Gon frowned. 'This spaceport is not going to be pleasant.'

Captain Panaka insisted. 'She is curious about the planet.'

Qui-Gon reluctantly agreed. 'Stay close to me,' he told Padmé. The little group soon arrived at the busy settlement of Mos Espa. The sandy streets were crowded with droids and aliens, hooded smugglers and scavenging Jawas.

Qui-Gon led them to a small junk shop owned by a dealer named Watto. With his leathery wings and dangling snout, Watto came from a species known as the Toydarians. He assured Qui-Gon that he had the right parts for his ship, and offered to take him outside for a look.

As Padmé waited inside the shop, she made a surprising new acquaintance. A young human boy was sitting on the counter, cleaning rusty spaceship parts. He asked Padmé if she was an angel – he'd never seen anyone so beautiful.

Costume concept for Handmaiden Padmé.
IAIN McCAIG / MARKER

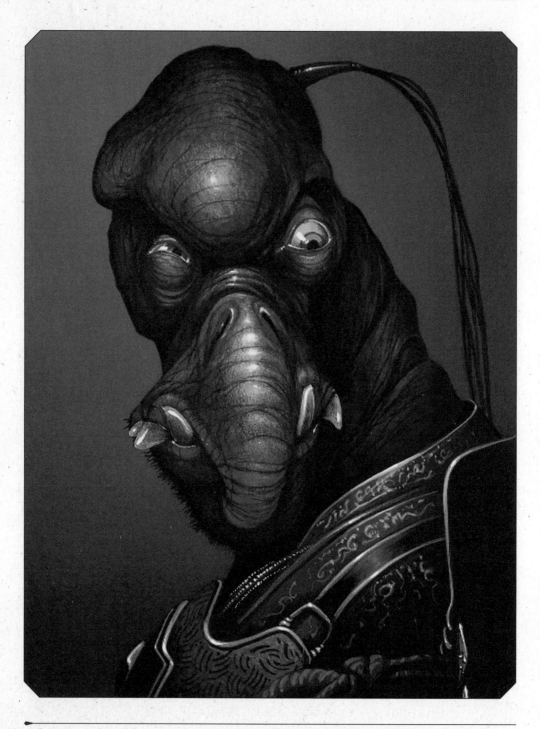

Concept art for the Toydarian merchant, Watto. **DOUG CHIANG / ACRYLIC PAINTING**

'You're a funny little boy,' Padmé said with a smile.

'I'm a pilot, you know,' he told her, 'and someday I'm gonna fly away from this place.' When that day would come, the boy did not know. The terrible truth was that he was enslaved, owned by Watto and forced to work in the Toydarian's shop. But he didn't want to be seen that way. 'I'm a person, and my name is Anakin.'

Outside in the junkyard, Qui-Gon was trying to use a Jedi mind trick to persuade Watto to hand over the parts he needed in return for Republic credits. But the trader refused. 'I'm a Toydarian. Mind tricks don't work on me – only money. No money, no parts!'

Qui-Gon had no choice but to walk away, taking Padmé and Jar Jar with him.

But wherever Jar Jar went, trouble soon followed. On the streets of Mos Espa, the clumsy Gungan found himself face to face with an angry Dug named Sebulba. Unexpectedly, he was rescued by young Anakin, who told Sebulba to back off.

Costume concept for Anakin Skywalker.
IAIN McCAIG / MARKER

'If you weren't a slave, I'd squash you right now,' Sebulba growled, but he let the boy and the Gungan go.

When a kindly old woman warned them that a sandstorm was coming, Anakin offered Qui-Gon and the others shelter. They arrived just in time and were introduced to Anakin's mother, Shmi Skywalker, who welcomed the strangers into her home.

Excitedly, Anakin showed Padmé his latest project: a half-finished protocol droid that he had named C-3PO. Though he was still unsteady on his feet, C-3PO wobbled over and introduced himself to the little astromech, R2-D2.

As the sandstorm raged outside, Shmi told her guests about her life working for Watto. Padmé was shocked. She thought the Republic had stamped out slavery. 'The Republic doesn't exist out here,' Shmi explained sadly. 'We must survive on our own.'

Anakin asked if they'd ever seen a podrace before. 'I'm the only human who can do it.'

Concept art for the Dug podracer, Sebulba. IAIN McCAIG / MARKER

'You must have Jedi reflexes if you race pods,' Qui-Gon responded.

'You're a Jedi Knight, aren't you?' Anakin asked. He had seen Qui-Gon's lightsaber and knew only Jedi carried that kind of weapon. Once, the little boy had dreamed that he was a Jedi, too. 'I came back here and freed all the slaves,' he told Qui-Gon. 'Have you come to free us?'

But Qui-Gon could only shake his head, and explain their real reason for being there: to find a new hyperdrive so they could reach Coruscant.

Concept art for C-3PO. **Doug Chiang / Air Marker**

'I can help!' Anakin offered. 'I can fix anything.' Qui-Gon didn't doubt it, but they didn't have the parts.

Shmi shared that gambling podraces was a weakness of the junk dealers. Anakin told them about the podracer he had built and offered to let Qui-Gon enter it into the big race on Boonta Eve if they made Watto believe it was theirs.

Shmi didn't want her son to take part in another dangerous podrace, but Anakin knew the prize money would more than pay for the parts they needed. He pleaded with her. 'Mom, you say that the biggest problem in the universe is nobody helps each other.'

Shmi sighed, realising that her son was right.

The next day, Qui-Gon returned to Watto's.

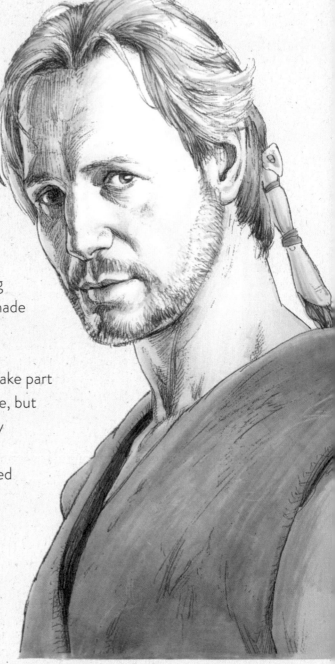

Costume concept for Qui-Gon Jinn. IAIN MCCAIG / MARKER

shop to strike a bargain. This time, the Toydarian was willing to listen, suggesting they split the winnings 50/50.

'I suggest you front the cash for the entry,' the Jedi said. 'If we win, you keep all the winnings, minus the cost of the parts I need. If we lose, you keep my ship.' Watto agreed. He thought Qui-Gon had made a foolish deal.

As Anakin and his friends worked to get his podracer ready, Qui-Gon spoke to the boy's mother. 'He has special powers. He can see things before they happen.' Shmi agreed. 'That's why he appears to have such quick reflexes,' Qui-Gon continued. 'It is a Jedi trait.'

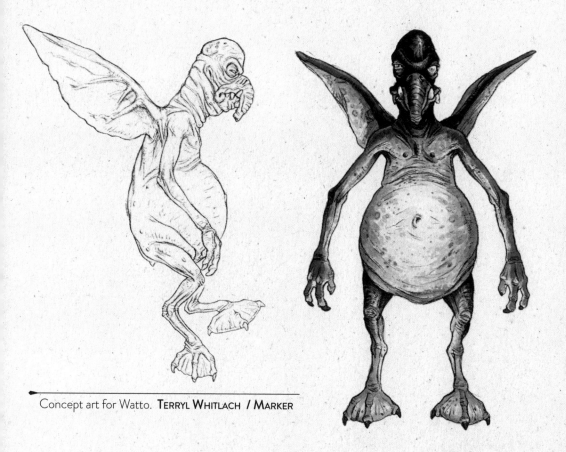

Concept art for Watto. TERRYL WHITLACH / MARKER

'He deserves better than a slave's life,' Shmi said.

'The Force is unusually strong with him,' Qui-Gon said. Still, he didn't know if he could help Anakin. 'I didn't actually come here to free slaves,' he admitted.

Soon, the podracer was ready to test. Anakin sat in the cockpit and fired up the two mighty engines attached to either side. 'It's working!' he said excitedly as the engines roared to life. Padmé, Qui-Gon and Shmi

Concept art for the Mos Espa Grand Arena featuring a podracer engine and an eopie being ridden. DOUG CHIANG / ACRYLIC PAINTING

watched with pride, and just a little uncertainty.

That night, a winged starship named the *Scimitar* landed in the deserts of Tatooine. The hatch lowered and the hooded figure of Darth Maul strode down onto the sand. He dispatched three flying probe droids to search the area for any sign of the Jedi. When he found them, he would destroy them, and take Queen Amidala.

The next morning was Boonta Eve, the day of the big podrace. The huge racing arena in Mos Espa was crowded with onlookers from across the Outer Rim. The conceited Dug, Sebulba, was the favourite to win.

'He always wins!' Watto told Qui-Gon Jinn. 'I'm betting heavily on Sebulba.'

Hearing that, Qui-Gon decided to offer Watto another deal. He wagered his new racing pod against the boy. If Anakin won, he would go free.

Watto laughed and agreed to Qui-Gon's bet. 'He won't win the race, so it makes little difference!'

Soon it was time for the podracers to be wheeled out onto the starting line. The other contestants included the famous Toong, Ben Quadinaros; the four-armed Xexto, Gasgano; and the long-snouted Glymphid, Aldar Beedo. But the loudest cheers were for Sebulba, who waved to the crowd as he headed for his podracer.

Before the race, Anakin's mother took her son aside and made him promise to be safe. Neither of them noticed Sebulba sneaking alongside, and loosening a vital part of Anakin's engine.

Concept art for the podracers, featuring Anakin Skywalker, Ben Quadinaros, Dud Bolt and Mars Guo. **TERRYL WHITLACH / PENCIL**

'You won't walk away from this one!' the Dug sneered.

But Anakin was determined to win the race, and the money Qui-Gon needed for the hyperdrive. 'Remember,' the Jedi Master told the boy. 'Concentrate on the moment. Feel, don't think. Use your instincts. And may the Force be with you.'

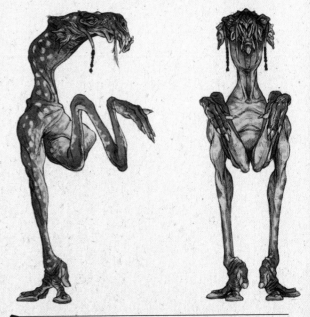

Concept art for Sebulba. **TERRYL WHITLACH / MARKER**

On a special platform overlooking the arena sat the most powerful of all local gangsters, the great slug-like creature known as Jabba the Hutt. He gestured to the crowd, welcoming them to the race.

Down on the track, the podracers roared into life. Anakin put on his goggles and flipped the starting switch. The noise of his engines was deafening.

Then Jabba gave the order, and the race was on.

Concept art for Jabba the Hutt. **IAIN MCCAIG / PENCIL**

Concept art for podracers. JOHN BELL / MARKER

The podracers rocketed over the starting line – all except two. Anakin's engine had stalled, and the crowd laughed as he struggled to get his racer moving. But Ben Quadinaros was even more unlucky: his podracer went completely to pieces, its four engines flying off in different directions.

At last, Anakin's engines reignited, and he shot across the starting line. But he was still far behind the others. Sebulba had already taken the lead, using his powerful podracer to slam the other contestants out of his way.

Anakin put on a burst of speed, and soon he could see the others ahead of him. As they emerged from a narrow canyon, he overtook the slowest racer and began moving up the pack.

He was startled when a bullet struck the cockpit, fired by one of the desert tribespeople known as Tuskens. They crouched on top of a stony ridge, screaming in triumph and waving their gaffi sticks in the air.

As the racers sped through the arena to begin another lap, Anakin was still in second-to-last position. But as they hurtled through the rocky terrain, he was able to pass first one and then another of his competitors, to claim third place.

Suddenly a shard of metal from an exploding podracer smashed into him! A cable on his own podracer came loose and his cockpit began to spin out of control. Three racers sped by, leaving Anakin dead last.

But the boy stayed calm, using a magnetic grabber to retrieve the cable and reattach it. Then he zoomed into another canyon, overtaking his rivals and getting into second place as they entered the final lap. Only Sebulba was ahead of him now.

Before long it was neck and neck, with first

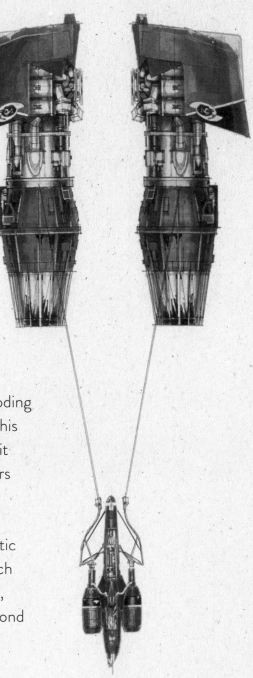

Concept art for podracer.
JAY SHUSTER / MARKER

Sebulba and then Anakin out in front. But the Dug wasn't about to give up easily. As the engine part he'd loosened on Anakin's podracer finally broke free, the boy was once again in trouble. Anakin's engines began to gush smoke, and he started to lose power.

Costume concept for Anakin Skywalker. **Iain McCaig / Pencil**

Again, Anakin reacted quickly. Transferring power from one engine to the other, he was able to pick up speed and catch Sebulba. By the final stretch they were flying side by side, each one trying to force the other into second place.

Sebulba slammed his podracer into Anakin's, over and over, trying to force him to crash, and the two craft became tangled together. Anakin saw his chance. Firing up his engines he boosted forward, tearing Sebulba's podracer to pieces. The Dug howled with fury as he spun uncontrollably into the sand.

Concept art for Anakin Skywalker's podracer. **Doug Chiang / Acrylic Painting**

Anakin Skywalker had won the race!

The crowd cheered wildly as he crossed the finish line. Qui-Gon lifted the boy onto his shoulder, and Anakin punched the air with excitement. 'Mom, I did it!'

Padmé hugged Anakin warmly. 'We owe you everything, Ani,' she said.

Shmi took her son in her arms. 'It's so wonderful, Ani. You have brought hope to those who have none. I'm so very proud of you.'

Qui-Gon went to find Watto and settle his debt. The Toydarian was furious, sure that he'd been cheated. Qui-Gon shook his head. 'Whenever you gamble, my friend, eventually you'll lose.' Watto had no choice but to release Anakin and hand over the parts Qui-Gon needed.

Qui-Gon took the new hyperdrive out to the Royal Starship. 'I'm going back,' he told Obi-Wan. 'Some unfinished business.'

Concept art for Watto. **DOUG CHIANG / DYE-SUBLIMATION PRINT**

Obi-Wan peered up at his master. 'Why do I sense we've picked up another pathetic life form?'

Back in Mos Espa, Qui-Gon and Anakin sold the boy's podracer and gave the money to Shmi. Then Qui-Gon revealed the truth. Thanks to his bargain with Watto, Anakin was free.

Shmi looked at Qui-Gon in amazement. 'Will you take him with you?' she asked. 'Is he to become a Jedi?'

Qui-Gon nodded. 'Yes, our meeting was not a coincidence. Nothing happens by accident.' Anakin was excited, but Qui-Gon warned him that becoming a Jedi was difficult – it was a hard life.

'But I want to go. It's what I've always dreamed of doing.' Anakin turned to his mother. 'Can I go, Mom?'

Shmi took her son's hand. 'Anakin, this path has been placed before you. The choice is yours alone.'

Excitedly, Anakin rushed off to pack his things. Then he realised something. 'You're coming with us, aren't you, Mom?'

Shmi shook her head. 'Son, my place is here. My future is here. It is time for you to let go.' She told Anakin she loved him, and the two embraced.

After a quick farewell to C-3PO, Anakin followed Qui-Gon out of the little dwelling. Shmi watched them go, kneeling as Anakin ran back for a final embrace. 'Will I ever see you again?' he asked tearfully.

Shmi smiled. 'What does your heart tell you?'

Anakin searched his feelings. He was unsure, but he had hope. 'I will come back and free you, Mom. I promise.'

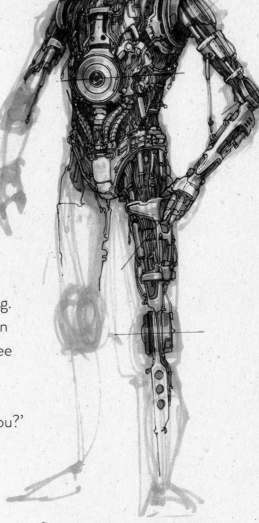

Concept art for C-3PO.
DOUG CHIANG / MARKER PEN

Concept art for the Naboo Royal Starship, featuring Darth Maul and Qui-Gon Jinn duelling.
DOUG CHIANG / ACRYLIC PAINTING

Then he turned away, and this time he didn't look back.

Out on the desert sands, Darth Maul's probe droids brought him the news he had been waiting for. Leaping aboard his speeder, the Sith warrior sped away across the dunes.

Darth Maul reached the Royal Starship just behind Qui-Gon and Anakin. The Jedi Master ordered the boy to take cover, then drew his lightsaber as Maul leapt from his speeder. The Sith Lord ignited his own laser sword, and battle was joined.

Anakin raced towards the ship as Qui-Gon and Darth Maul fought, their blades clashing furiously. Obi-Wan ordered Ric Olié to take off and fly low over the dunes with the ramp lowered. As the ship passed overhead Qui-Gon used the Force to leap onto the ramp, leaving Darth Maul standing furiously on the sand.

Back on the Royal Starship, Qui-Gon paused to catch his breath. His opponent had been well trained in the Jedi arts. 'My guess is it was after the queen,' he told Obi-Wan.

Then he introduced his Padawan to the newest member of their little band. 'Anakin Skywalker, meet Obi-Wan Kenobi.'

The pair shook hands, little knowing how much each of them would change the other's life from that day forward.

That night, Padmé couldn't sleep. She was too afraid for her people back on Naboo. In the starship's living quarters she came across Anakin Skywalker, who was shivering from the cold.

Padmé fetched the boy a blanket and came to sit beside him. Anakin gave the young handmaiden a gift he'd made for her: a good luck charm carved from a snippet of a substance called japor, for her to remember him by.

She would still be there for Anakin when they reached the capital, but knew that he missed his mother and was feeling all alone in the galaxy.

Soon the Royal Starship arrived at the city-world of Coruscant, where they found Senator Palpatine and Supreme Chancellor Valorum waiting. The two politicians greeted Queen Amidala, and expressed their relief at her safe arrival.

Qui-Gon and Obi-Wan bowed respectfully to Chancellor Valorum. 'I must speak with the Jedi Council immediately,' Qui-Gon informed him. 'The situation has become much more complicated.'

Queen Amidala led the way to an air taxi, and Anakin followed. The floating vehicle soared out across the endless city, weaving between huge skyscrapers and gleaming silver towers until they came to Senator Palpatine's quarters.

Once inside, the queen spoke frankly. 'Our people are dying,' she told Senator Palpatine. 'We must do something quickly to stop the Federation.'

But Palpatine was not hopeful. He feared that the other senators would take too long to reach a decision. 'Our best choice would be to push for the election of a stronger Supreme Chancellor,' he said. 'One who will take control, enforce the laws and give us justice.'

Meanwhile, Qui-Gon and Obi-Wan had travelled to the Jedi Temple, a magnificent building topped with a crown of five shining spires. In a special chamber atop the highest tower, the Jedi Council had gathered to hear his report. Among them were many powerful Jedi including the mighty warrior, Mace Windu; the wise Cerean, Ki-Adi Mundi; and the oldest and most respected of all the Jedi: Grand Master Yoda.

Qui-Gon began by telling the council about the lightsaber-wielding foe he had encountered on Tatooine. 'My only conclusion can be that it was a Sith Lord.'

A murmur of surprise went around the council chamber. 'The Sith have been extinct for a millennium,' argued Ki-Adi Mundi.

But Master Yoda wasn't so sure. 'Hard to see, the dark side is.'

Qui-Gon then turned to the other matter that concerned him. 'I have encountered a vergence in the Force. It's centred around a boy. I request that he be tested.'

Concept art for the city-planet of Coruscant. **DOUG CHIANG / DYE-SUBLIMATION PRINT**

Mace Windu agreed. 'Bring him before us, then.'

Inside the huge domed Senate building, delegates from hundreds of worlds gathered in their floating repulsorpods. Fearlessly, Queen Amidala informed the senators that her home world of Naboo had been invaded and occupied by the Trade Federation and their droid army.

The representative from the Trade Federation reacted angrily, calling her a liar. He demanded that the Supreme Chancellor send an observer to Naboo, to discover the truth. Queen Amidala knew that could take weeks.

Concept art for Yoda. IAIN McCAIG / MARKER

She faced the senators angrily. 'I was not elected to watch my people suffer and die while you discuss this invasion in a committee,' she snapped. 'I suggest new leadership is needed. I move for a vote of no confidence in Chancellor Valorum.'

The Senate erupted. Many senators defended

the Supreme Chancellor, while others sided with Queen Amidala. It was decided that the vote would be taken the following day.

'They will elect a new chancellor,' Senator Palpatine told the queen confidently. 'A strong chancellor, who will not let our tragedy continue.'

As the sun set over the Jedi Temple, Anakin stood before Master Yoda and the Jedi Council. He had been put through a series of challenges to decide if he was worthy to become a Jedi. Now the testing was almost over.

Ki-Adi Mundi inspected the boy closely. 'Your thoughts dwell on your mother,' he observed.

Concept art for an alien senator.
IAIN MCCAIG / MARKER

Master Yoda nodded in agreement. 'Afraid to lose her, I think.'

Anakin frowned. 'What's that got to do with anything?' he asked.

Master Yoda leaned forward, fixing the boy with a powerful stare. 'Everything,' he said. 'Fear is the path to the dark side. Fear leads to anger. Anger leads to hate. Hate leads to suffering. I sense much fear in you.'

Anakin said nothing, and waited to see how his fate would be decided.

Back in Senator Palpatine's quarters, Queen Amidala at last received some good news. Among several other candidates, Palpatine had been nominated to succeed Supreme Chancellor Valorum.

'A surprise, to be sure,' Palpatine said, 'but a welcome one. The Trade Federation will lose its influence and our people will be freed.'

The queen was unwilling to wait that long. 'I have decided to go back to Naboo.'

Palpatine was horrified. 'Please, Your Majesty. Stay here, where it's safe.'

But the queen's mind was made up. She was determined to re-join her people.

At the Jedi Temple, Qui-Gon Jinn and Obi-Wan Kenobi had joined Anakin in the council chamber. The Jedi were ready to announce their decision.

'He will not be trained,' Mace Windu told them. 'He is too old.'

Qui-Gon shook his head. 'I will train him, then. I will take Anakin as my Padawan learner.'

Concept art for the Jedi Master Oppo Rancisis.
IAIN McCAIG / MARKER

'An apprentice you have,' Master Yoda pointed out. 'Impossible, to take on a second.'

'There is little more he can learn from me,' Qui-Gon said of Obi-Wan. Obi-Wan agreed, saying he was ready to take the trials to become a Jedi Knight.

'Now is not the time for this,' Mace Windu said. 'Queen Amidala is returning home. Go with her to Naboo and discover the identity of this dark warrior. This is the clue we need to unravel this mystery of the Sith.'

Qui-Gon bowed to Grand Master Yoda, then left the chamber with Anakin and Obi-Wan.

But as they headed to the Royal Starship for their journey back to Naboo, Obi-Wan expressed his own doubts about young Anakin. 'The boy is dangerous,' he told Qui-Gon. 'The council sense it. Why can't you?'

'His fate is uncertain, not dangerous,' Qui-Gon responded. 'The council will decide Anakin's future. Now get on board.'

Concept art for Yoda. **IAIN McCAIG / MARKER**

Moments later, Queen Amidala arrived at the landing platform with her handmaidens and bodyguards. Qui-Gon welcomed her, offering his protection when they reached Naboo. But if the young queen was afraid, she showed no sign of it.

Jar Jar Binks was giddy to be going home. He led Anakin and R2-D2 up the ramp and the Royal Starship took off, leaving Coruscant far behind.

In the Royal Palace on Naboo, Viceroy Gunray was making another report to Darth Sidious. The planet was now entirely in the hands of the Trade Federation – even the city of the Gungans.

Sidious was pleased. 'Good. I am sending my apprentice, Darth Maul, to join you.' The viceroy was surprised, but had no choice. The Sith were too powerful.

On the Royal Starship's bridge, Ric Olié was teaching Anakin how to use the controls. The boy was eager to learn. He'd always wanted to become a pilot.

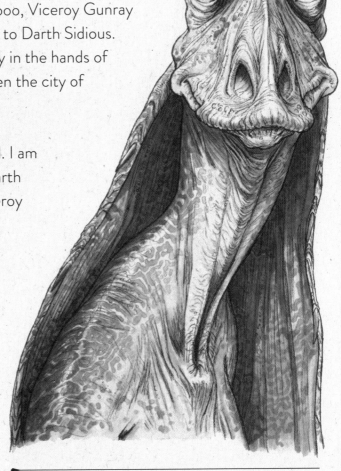

Concept art for Jar Jar Binks. **Terryl Whitlach / Marker**

But in the queen's chamber, Captain Panaka was filled with concern. 'The moment we land, the Federation will arrest you,' he told her. 'We have no army!'

Qui-Gon Jinn agreed. 'I can only protect you. I can't fight a war for you.'

To everyone's surprise, the queen called out the name of Jar Jar Binks. The Gungan looked up. He wasn't sure what to say. But the queen beckoned to him. 'I need your help.'

Slipping past the Trade Federation battleships, the Royal Starship landed in the forests of Naboo. Jar Jar Binks set off for Gunga City to find his people, while the rest of the group waited for him to return.

Obi-Wan took this chance to apologize for the way he'd spoken to Qui-Gon back on Coruscant. 'It's not my place to disagree with you about the boy.'

Qui-Gon smiled. 'You're a much wiser man than I am, Obi-Wan. I foresee you will become a great Jedi Knight.'

But when Jar Jar Binks returned from Gunga City, he came with bad news. His home was deserted, and there were signs of a fight.

Qui-Gon feared that the Gungans had been rounded up by the Trade Federation, but Jar Jar didn't think so. He told them that in times of trouble, the Gungans would flee to their sacred place. 'Come on!'

They found the Gungans hiding in the ruins of an ancient temple deep in the forest. Queen Amidala and Jar Jar Binks were taken before Boss Nass.

Costume concept for 'Handmaiden' Padmé. **Iain McCaig / Marker**

He wasn't happy to see them. He blamed the queen and her people for bringing the battle droids to Naboo, and putting the Gungans in danger.

'I come before you in peace,' the queen said. 'We wish to form an alliance.'

But before she could say any more, the handmaiden Padmé stepped forward.

'I am Queen Amidala,' she said, to the amazement of all those gathered around her. Anakin gasped in surprise, and even the Jedi were taken aback.

'This is my decoy,' Padmé went on, gesturing to the young woman dressed like the queen. 'I am sorry for my deception, but it was necessary to protect myself.'

She faced Boss Nass. 'Our two great societies have always lived in peace,' she reminded the powerful Gungan. 'Now I beg you to help us.'

The young queen got down on her knees. Anakin and the others did the same, kneeling on a carpet of dry leaves. 'Our fate is in your hands,' Padmé said.

Boss Nass laughed proudly, his great jowls quivering. He had always believed that the human population of Naboo thought themselves better than the Gungans. Now, Queen Amidala herself had proved that wasn't true. He agreed to make an alliance.

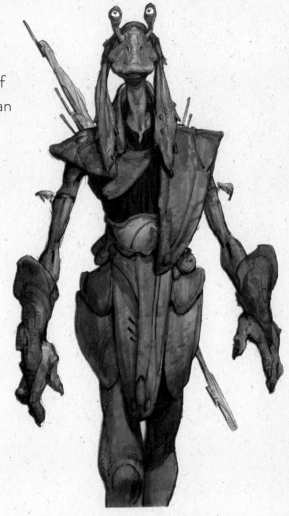

On the plains of Naboo, Captain Panaka had made contact with those few loyal citizens who had been able to escape the Trade Federation. But even with the aid of the Gungans, the captain knew that they were vastly outnumbered. 'I do not think this is a battle we can win,' he told the queen.

'The battle is only a diversion,' the queen informed him. 'The Gungans must draw the droid army away from the city, so we can enter the palace and capture the viceroy.'

Costume concept for Gungans.
IAIN MCCAIG / MARKER

Qui-Gon was doubtful. 'There is a possibility that many Gungans will be killed.'

But the queen had a plan for that, too. 'We will send our pilots to knock out the Droid Control Ship orbiting the planet. Then the droids will be helpless.'

Inside the Royal Palace, Darth Maul had joined Viceroy Gunray. They informed Darth Sidious about the army gathering in the swamps, but the Viceroy was sure that his droids would be able to defeat the Gungans easily.

However, Darth Sidious demanded more than just a victory. 'Wipe them out,' he said cruelly. 'All of them!'

Hidden among clouds of fog, the Gungan army marched through the swamp. With them were huge, lizard-like creatures named fambaas, with shield generators mounted on their backs. As they emerged onto the grassy plains, the Gungans fired up the generators to form a protective dome around their army.

No one knew how long the shield could hold against the might of the attacking battle droids. Jar Jar Binks, now a general in the Gungan army, watched in terror as the vast troop transports rumbled into view.

The droid army opened fire, their huge cannons blasting the Gungan shield. For now, the shield stood firm.

Costume concept for Gungan warriors.
TONY WRIGHT /
GOUACHE MARKER

In the city of Theed, Queen Amidala and the Jedi were hiding from a droid patrol. Qui-Gon took

Anakin aside. 'Once we get inside, you find a safe place to hide and stay there.' The boy promised to do as he was told.

Captain Panaka's team opened fire on the droids, creating a distraction so Queen Amidala and the Jedi could slip into the Royal Palace. They headed for the main hangar, destroying the droids on duty so the Naboo pilots could get to their ships.

Concept art of Gungan warriors riding kaadu on Naboo's Great Grass Plains. **DOUG CHIANG / ACRYLIC PAINTING**

Led by Ric Olié, the tiny Naboo fleet took off, heading into orbit to attack the Droid Control Ship. They soon ran into a much larger swarm of enemy fighters. Before long, the darkness of space was lit by laser bolts and explosions.

In the throne room, Viceroy Gunray gave the order to activate the entire droid army. As the Gungan soldiers watched, thousands of battle droids unfolded from their troop transports, drew their weapons and began to march across the plain.

Concept art for Trade Federation AAT battle tanks.
DOUG CHIANG / MARKER

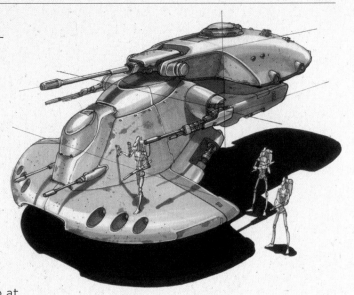

The Gungan shields had been designed to withstand blaster fire, not droids. The battle droids pushed through the protective screen and began to fire at the Gungans. Jar Jar and the others defended themselves with spears and energy catapults, using their slings to hurl exploding spheres known as boomas towards the enemy. But still the droids kept coming.

With blaster fire erupting all around the Royal Palace's main hangar, Anakin and R2-D2 took shelter in one of the empty Naboo fighter ships. Qui-Gon ordered the boy to stay in the cockpit and keep out of danger.

But as the Jedi headed for the throne room, they were confronted by a terrifying sight. Darth Maul stood in the doorway wearing a black cloak and hood.

'We'll handle this,' Qui-Gon told Queen Amidala. Obi-Wan joined his master, and the Jedi ignited their lightsabers.

Darth Maul threw back his hood to reveal a head spiked with fearsome horns. He drew his lightsaber, activating not one but two crimson blades. Then the Sith Lord leapt forward, and the sound of clashing blades filled the stone chamber.

Across the hangar, the queen and her people were pinned down by three shielded droidekas. Anakin was eager to help, fumbling with the fighter's controls as he tried to work out where the main guns were.

Instead the ship took off, floating slowly out of the hangar. Anakin found the guns and blasted the droidekas, allowing the queen and the others to escape. But he was stuck in the cockpit, and the ship was still moving.

'It's on automatic pilot!' he told R2-D2 as the ship spiralled up above the planet and into the darkness of space. He could see the Droid Control Ship in the distance, and the Naboo fighters circling around it.

Anakin ordered R2-D2 to deactivate the automatic pilot and took control of the ship himself. As enemy fighters sped closer Anakin swooped and spun, using his Jedi skills to stay one step ahead. 'Qui-Gon told me to stay in this cockpit,' he told R2-D2, 'and that's what I'm gonna do!'

Costume concept for Darth Maul.
IAIN McCAIG / MARKER

Back at the palace, Qui-Gon Jinn and Obi-Wan Kenobi pursued Darth Maul into the central power plant, a maze of metal walkways and humming electrical generators. The Sith Lord was able to throw Obi-Wan down, knocking his lightsaber from his hand. But Qui-Gon pressed the attack, driving Maul into a corridor lined with pulsing electric beams.

Temporarily separated from Maul by the beams, Qui-Gon closed his eyes, gathering his strength for the battle. Trapped outside the corridor, Obi-Wan could only watch as his master prepared to face Maul alone.

On the plains of Naboo, the Gungan army were losing. Their shield had fallen and they'd been forced to retreat, with the droid army in pursuit. Jar Jar and the others tried to fight back, but it wasn't long before they were captured.

In the palace, the same fate awaited Queen Amidala. She and her troops were surrounded by droidekas, and she saw no choice but to lay down her weapon. Their only hope was that the fighters would be able to knock out the Droid Control Ship and shut down the droid army.

Concept art for R2-D2, showing his utility arms.
DOUG CHIANG / MARKER PEN

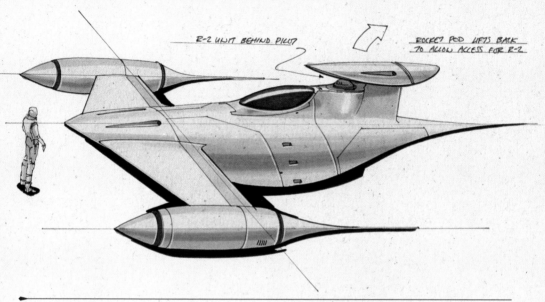

R-2 UNIT BEHIND PILOT

ROCKET POD LIFTS BACK TO ALLOW ACCESS FOR R-2

Concept art for the Naboo starfighter. **Doug Chiang / Marker**

But as Anakin prepared to engage the Federation battleship, his fighter was hit by enemy fire. Struggling for control, he found himself spinning closer and closer to the battleship's docking bay. He finally screeched to a halt inside the battleship's hangar. His ship had lost power, and battle droids were approaching from every side.

In the power station, Darth Maul and Qui-Gon Jinn had resumed their battle. But as Obi-Wan raced to his master's aid, something dreadful happened. Smashing Qui-Gon with the handle of his lightsaber, Darth Maul spun and sank the blade deep into the Jedi Master's chest. Qui-Gon fell, and Obi-Wan cried out in horror.

Struggling to control his feelings of rage and grief, Obi-Wan swung his lightsaber at Darth Maul. The pair fought furiously, their gleaming blades clashing. Obi-Wan was able to sever Darth Maul's double-bladed lightsaber, but it wasn't enough. The Sith Lord drove the young Jedi back

Costume concept for Darth Maul. **Iain McCaig / Marker**

into a deep pit, leaving him dangling over the abyss.

But Obi-Wan wasn't defeated. Using the Force, he snatched up Qui-Gon's lightsaber and leapt from the pit, startling Darth Maul. With a powerful slice of his saber he destroyed his enemy, and Maul fell down into the pit.

Obi-Wan ran to Qui-Gon's side, holding his master's head in his hands. 'Promise me you will train the boy,' Qui-Gon said with his dying breaths. Then his eyes closed and he spoke no more.

Inside the Droid Control Ship, Anakin had managed to get his fighter's power supply running again. But as he tried to shoot at the droids marching towards him, the boy accidentally blasted the battleship's main reactor core. The vast ship began to explode, and Anakin was barely able to escape before it tore itself to pieces in a spectacular explosion.

With their control ship gone, the droid army lost power. The Gungans cheered as

Costume concept for Obi-Wan Kenobi. **IAIN McCAIG / MARKER**

their enemy collapsed to the ground. In the throne room, Queen Amidala drew her blaster and aimed it at Viceroy Gunray. The war had been won.

In the days that followed, Queen Amidala reclaimed her throne and began to repair some of the damage wrought by the Trade Federation. Senator Palpatine had been elected to the post of Supreme Chancellor, and the queen was proud to welcome him back to Naboo.

Concept art for the Battle of Naboo, featuring Trade Federation battleships and a Naboo N-1 starfighter. DOUG CHIANG / ACRYLIC PAINTING

'Your boldness has saved our people, Your Majesty,' Palpatine said proudly. 'Together, we shall bring peace and prosperity to the Republic.'

Several Jedi had also made the journey to Naboo, among them Mace Windu and Grand Master Yoda. The Jedi Council had voted to grant Obi-Wan Kenobi the title of Jedi Knight, but Yoda urged caution when it came to the matter of Anakin Skywalker.

Banner from the royal palace. **KURT KAUFMAN / MARKER**

'Master Yoda, I gave Qui-Gon my word,' Obi-Wan insisted. 'I will train Anakin. Without the approval of the council if I must.'

Yoda sighed. 'Agree, the council does. Your apprentice, young Skywalker will be.'

As night fell, it was time to bid farewell to Qui-Gon Jinn. In a funeral temple on Naboo his body was given to the flames, as Queen Amidala, Supreme Chancellor Palpatine and many others watched sorrowfully.

'There's no doubt the mysterious warrior was a Sith,' Mace Windu told Master Yoda. They both knew that only a powerful being could have defeated someone as strong in the Force as Qui-Gon Jinn.

Yoda nodded. 'Always two there are. A master and an apprentice.'

Mace Windu gazed into the flames. 'But which one was destroyed?' he wondered.

To celebrate Naboo's victory, Queen Amidala threw a great parade through the streets of Theed. Led by Boss Nass and Jar Jar Binks, the Gungan army marched through the city, surrounded by a huge, cheering crowd. Thanks to them, the Trade Federation had been defeated and the planet was free once more.

As Boss Nass approached, Queen Amidala held out a glowing globe to symbolise a new era of peace and understanding between their peoples. Anakin Skywalker stood beside his new master, Obi-Wan Kenobi, watching the celebrations.

He had no idea what the future might hold, but he knew it would be filled with adventure.

Concept art for the city of Theed, capital of Naboo. **KURT KAUFMAN / MARKER**

Artists

Concept art for the opee sea killer. **DOUG CHIANG / DYE-SUBLIMATION PRINT**

DOUG CHIANG was born in Taipei and studied film at UCLA and industrial design at Detroit's College for Creative Studies. Chiang joined Industrial Light & Magic as a creative director and contributed to ILM's visual effects efforts on *Terminator 2: Judgment Day, Jumanji, Ghost, Forrest Gump,* and more. In the late 1990s Chiang joined Lucasfilm as design director on *Star Wars* Episode I: *The Phantom Menace* and continued there as concept design supervisor on Episode II: *Attack of the Clones* and many more *Star Wars* projects. Among Chiang's professional accolades is an Academy Award for *Death Becomes Her* and a FOCUS Award for his independent film, *Mental Block*.

IAIN MCCAIG is an award-winning artist, screenwriter and filmmaker, and a leading conceptual designer with an impressive command of human anatomy and emotional expression. McCaig worked for Lucasfilm as a principal designer on all three of the *Star Wars* prequels, developing the famous looks of characters including Queen Amidala and Darth Maul. Among McCaig's other film credits are *Terminator 2: Judgment Day*, *Hook*, *Harry Potter and the Goblet of Fire* and *Guardians of the Galaxy*. McCaig's work has appeared in advertisements and children's books and on book and record covers, including the iconic artwork used on the classic Jethro Tull release *The Broadsword and the Beast*.

ED NATIVIDAD majored in transportation design at Detroit's College for Creative Studies and interned at Ford and General Motors before employing his illustrative talents to become an acclaimed conceptual artist. Natividad's filmography includes *Forrest Gump*, *Indiana Jones and the Kingdom of the Crystal Skull*, *I Am Legend*, *Transformers*, *Man of Steel*, *The Amazing Spider-Man*, and *Guardians of the Galaxy Vol. 3*. While working on the *Star Wars* prequels, Natividad came up with dimly lit Coruscant streetscapes, bone-dry Geonosian alleyways, and other examples of immersive environmental design.

BRIAN FLORA joined Industrial Light and Magic in 1988 as an assistant matte artist, learning traditional matte painting skills that he would go on to use in films such as *Batman Returns*, *Hocus Pocus*, and *Starship Troopers*. Having transitioned to digital painting, Flora returned to Industrial Light and Magic in 1996, where he rose to the position of senior matte artist and created some of the most iconic imagery seen in *Star Wars* Episode I: *The Phantom Menace*. He has gone on to create concept art and matte paintings for many blockbuster films, including *The Matrix Reloaded* and *The Matrix Revolutions*, *The Polar Express*, *Sin City* and *Looper*.

TERRYL WHITLACH is one of the top creature designers in the world today, bringing an in-depth knowledge of animal anatomy to the concept art process. With formal training in both art and zoology, Whitlach created art and illustrations for zoos and wildlife charities before being invited by Industrial Light and Magic to contribute to the animal designs in *Jumanji*. Doug Chiang then hired her to design most of the new creatures for *Star Wars* Episode I: *The Phantom Menace*. She is the author of *The Wildlife of Star Wars: A Field Guide*, with Bob Carrau, and has taught Creature Design and Construction/Anatomy at the Academy of Art University in San Francisco.

JOHN BELL was fascinated by cars from an early age, and after receiving a degree in Transportation Design from Art Center in Pasadena, he went to work at the General Motors Advanced Concept Studio in Detroit, and later became a concept artist at Atari Games in California. In the late 1980s, Bell joined Industrial Light and Magic, where he worked as an illustrator and art director. His filmography includes classics like *Star Trek IV: The Voyage Home*, *Back to the Future II* and *III*, and *Jurassic Park*. Most recently he contributed concept art designs for *Rogue One: A Star Wars Story*.

JAY SHUSTER is a third-generation artist and designer with a keen interest in planes, trains and automobiles, who studied product design at the Center for Creative Studies College of Art Design in Detroit. After a brief career in video games, Shuster began freelancing for Industrial Light and Magic, and was hired as a storyboard artist for *Star Wars* Episode I: *The Phantom Menace* in 1996, to which he also contributed concept art. In 2002, after working on *Star Wars* Episode II: *Attack of the Clones*, Shuster joined Pixar, where he has designed characters and environments for films like *Cars*, *Wall·E* and *The Incredibles*.

TONY WRIGHT is an illustrator from London whose work, under the pseudonym RIOT INK, has appeared in many different publications including *Melody Maker*, *Time Out*, *The Times*, the *Observer*, and the *Mirror*. He has also worked extensively as a storyboard and concept artist on films like *Star Wars* Episode I: *The Phantom Menace*, *The Talented Mr Ripley*, *Harry Potter and the Sorcerer's Stone*, *The English Patient* and *Lost in Space*.

KURT KAUFMAN studied Transportation Design at the Art Center College of Design in Pasadena and was introduced to legendary designer and concept artist Syd Mead, whom he cites as a major inspiration for his career in movies. His first film project as an illustrator was on *Robocop*, and in 1990 he was hired by Industrial Light and Magic to work on *Hook*. At ILM he met art director Doug Chiang, whom he would go on to work with on *Death Becomes Her*. Chiang later hired him to work as a storyboard and concept artist on *Star Wars* Episodes I and II. As a matte artist, he has worked on films such as *Jurassic Park III* and *Gangs of New York*.

Concept art for the Tatooine podrace course. DOUG CHIANG / DYE-SUBLIMATION PRINT

Concept art for Coruscant. **Doug Chiang / Dye-Sublimation Print**